5 SCARY STORIES FOR A DARK KNIGHT

BATMAN
5 SCARY STORIES
FOR A DARK KNIGHT

By Cavan Scott

Illustrated by Jeannette Arroyo

Batman created by Bob Kane with Bill Finger

Random House New York

Published in the United States by Random House Children's Books, a division
of Penguin Random House LLC, 1745 Broadway, New York, NY 10019, and in
Canada by Penguin Random House Canada Limited, Toronto. Random House and
the colophon are registered trademarks of Penguin Random House LLC.

ISBN 978-0-593-48398-5 (hc) — ISBN 978-0-593-48399-2 (lib. bdg.)
ISBN 978-0-593-48400-5 (ebook)

Printed in the United States of America

10 9 8 7 6 5 4 3 2 1

Random House Children's Books supports the First Amendment and
celebrates the right to read.

CONTENTS

Hello?

Oh, it's you. I've been expecting
you for quite some time, although how you slipped past
the Batcave's security system is a mystery.

Perhaps you're a ghost. Ha, ha. Nothing would surprise me.

Who am I? Oh, I do beg your pardon. I haven't introduced
myself. How remiss of me. My name is Alfred Pennyworth,
loyal butler to Bruce Wayne and right-hand man to . . .
well, you know who.

He has collected so many names over
the years. The Dark Knight. The Caped Crusader.
Batman.

You'll forgive me if I work as we talk, won't you?
The Batcave gets so dusty, and I do like everything
to be spick-and-span.

This part of the cave is the master's trophy room—
although, between you and me, I have no idea why he insists
on keeping so many ghastly mementos of his past adventures.

Take this painting, for example. Not my cup
of tea at all, especially when you consider its
sinister history.

Hmm? You haven't heard of it?

The Witch's Trap? Oh, it's positively bloodcurdling. Every one of these knick-knacks has a story to tell, and this one is no different. I could tell you the tale, if you want. It concerns that feline femme fatale, the villainous Catwoman.

It all began on a dark and stormy night... as most stories set in Gotham City invariably do....

ONE

PICTURE IMPURRRFECT

Catwoman was on the prowl, jumping from roof to roof as the rain poured down. She didn't mind the weather. This was one cat who wasn't scared of a little water, especially when she had her heart set on a prize.

News had reached her of a private art collection on Gotham City's West Side, the glittering playground of the city's rich and powerful, with its gleaming skyscrapers and luxury apartments.

Here, those with money thought they were safe from the city's criminal community. Selina Kyle was about to show one unfortunate citizen how wrong they were.

She found the apartment in no time, waiting patiently on a neighboring rooftop for its occupant to go out for the evening. Catwoman tensed as a limo pulled up in front of the building, and her

mark immediately dashed out to it, the collar of his coat turned up against the cold. She watched, the long car's glowing headlights disappearing into the gathering fog. Then she struck.

Yes, the spacious apartment, with its priceless collection of paintings and trinkets, had a security system, an extremely sophisticated one at that, but there wasn't an alarm in Gotham City that

Catwoman couldn't deactivate. She was inside within seconds, padding from room to room until she found what she was looking for. Her informer had told her about one particular painting, a rare piece that was worth more than any other work in the collection: *The Witch's Trap*, a masterpiece talked about in hushed tones by collectors and critics alike. A masterpiece very few people had ever seen.

And there it was, taking pride of place in the owner's study. A portrait, framed above a mahogany desk.

A portrait that was . . . hideous. Grotesque.

Is this it? Catwoman thought, staring at the canvas, a shiver of disgust running down her spine. *Who in their right mind would want* this *watching over them?*

The portrait was of a young woman, barely older than Catwoman herself. She had raven hair and shocking blue eyes that were wide with fright and rage. Most portraits showed their subjects sitting motionless, staring calmly out of the canvas, but this woman was screaming, her palms facing out as if pressed against glass. She looked for all the world like a prisoner within the frame, desperate to escape. Catwoman knew what that felt like from her time locked up in Blackgate Penitentiary. She had vowed never to be behind bars again, which meant never getting caught.

She needed to move. The longer she remained here, staring at the picture, the more chance there was that she would be discovered. Then why did she hesitate? Why hadn't she already snatched the painting from the wall and slipped back out into the night?

Because her skin was crawling beneath her catsuit. There was something about the painting that made her feel nervous and unnerved—repulsed, even—a sixth sense warning her that something wasn't right.

But that was stupid. She was Catwoman. Stealing jewelry and paintings was second nature. She'd been doing it since she was a kitten. Besides, she didn't have to like a portrait to get rich selling it on the black market.

Not wanting to stare into those haunted eyes a moment longer, Catwoman carefully lifted the frame from its hook and prepared to make her exit.

That was when she heard the voice, an eerie rasp like a dry brush being dragged across canvas.

Freee meeeeeeee.

Catwoman cried out in shock, dropping the painting. The frame clattered to the floor and Catwoman half expected the noise to bring Batman smashing through the window. She waited, breathing heavily, but no one came. Not the store owner returning early, and not the Bat.

Good. She had wasted enough time.

Recovering the frame, she was about to leave, when she noticed something that made her hiss with annoyance. The portrait had been damaged in the fall, a small tear in the canvas across one of the young woman's palms. Could it be repaired? Gingerly, Catwoman examined the rip with one of her claws. Maybe it wasn't that bad after all.

Oh, how wrong she was.

Catwoman cried out in surprise as a pale hand burst out of the painting, ice-cold fingers closing tight around her wrist.

She struggled, trying to pull away, but the hand wouldn't let go. Her eyes met those of the woman in the painting, and Catwoman screamed.

Batman's eyes narrowed when he saw *The Witch's Trap* later that night. He had been called to the private collection by Commissioner Gordon when the owner had raised the alarm, returning home to find the security system deactivated. Nothing had been taken, not even *The Witch's Trap*, although the portrait had been thrown on the floor of the study.

But that wasn't the most disturbing thing. The portrait had changed.

Gone was the picture of the raven-haired woman trying to escape. In her place was Cat-woman, captured in the same exact pose, gloved hands pressed against the canvas and a silent scream on her lips.

PICTURE IMPURRFECT

"What do you think?" Commissioner Gordon asked.

"It's a startling likeness," Batman said, looking grimly at the tortured portrait of his sometimes friend, sometimes rival.

"But it shouldn't look like that," the owner said, wringing his hands. "*The Witch's Trap* shows a young woman with black hair. *This* is obviously *not* the original."

"Could Catwoman have swapped the real portrait for this . . . fake?" Gordon wondered aloud.

"But why leave a clue to her crime?" Batman asked. "Selina isn't The Riddler. And if this *is* a forgery—"

"It's an extraordinary one," the owner confirmed. "The brushwork . . . the colors . . . They perfectly match the original. If I didn't know better, I would say the portrait was painted over two hundred years ago."

"Who *was* the original artist?" Batman asked.

"Augustus Nightstorm," the owner replied, looking pleased that he knew something the

World's Greatest Detective did not. "An old seventeenth-century Gothamite with a somewhat shady reputation."

"Shady how?" Gordon asked.

"He was rumored to have dabbled in the occult. Witchcraft. Sorcery. Arcane knowledge. That kind of thing."

"Hence *The Witch's Trap*," the commissioner said. "Do we know who the woman was? In the original, I mean."

The owner shook his head. "No one knows for sure. Some people say her name was Hilda . . . Hilda Grimling, I think, but that's as far as the stories go."

"Not much to go on," Jim Gordon said, rubbing the back of his neck as he turned to Batman. "Do *you* know anything about the painting?"

"No," Batman admitted, still examining the canvas. "But the name of the artist is familiar."

"Augustus Nightstorm?"

Batman nodded. "There's an art dealer with the same surname who has a gallery in the

Downtown area of Gotham City, just across from the Narrows."

The owner raised his eyebrows. "Are you a collector yourself, Batman?"

The Dark Knight didn't answer. It would have been too complicated to explain that his alter ego, billionaire Bruce Wayne, had met a curious man by the name of Theodore Nightstorm at a charity gala not long before. The art dealer had certainly left an impression, with his long beaklike nose and shock of bright red hair. And then there had been the strange pendant he wore—a human eye enclosed in a five-pointed star. Something told him that the young man would be able to shed some light on both the original painting and this impressive fake. If it was a fake at all.

Batman could almost hear Selina's cries for help as he looked into her painted eyes. Was she in trouble? Was the painting some kind of bizarre ransom note?

"Could I borrow this?" he asked, holding up the portrait. "For the investigation."

"Be my guest," the owner replied, glancing at where the original had hung on the wall. "It's fake—no use to me."

When he looked back again, Batman was gone.

"He does that," Commissioner Gordon told him with a weary smile. "You get used to it . . . eventually."

It didn't take Batman long to track down Theodore Nightstorm's gallery in the twisting maze of avenues and alleyways that made up Gotham City's Narrows. The gallery's metal shutters were down, but they did little to muffle the sudden sound of a scream coming from inside the building. With no way past the shutters, Batman climbed up to the first floor, the portrait slung over his back, and jimmied open the window.

There were more screams, even louder now, shrill and full of fear. Batman moved silently through the storeroom on the upper level, and swept down the stairs, finding himself in an office. The door, which led into the gallery, stood ajar, and Batman could hear that same scared voice, pleading between screams.

"Please. Don't hurt me. It's not my fault."

Batman crept forward and peered through the gap in the door, his eyes going wide beneath his mask.

The gallery was a wide, elegant space, its walls lined with expensive paintings and intricate sculptures. On one tall pedestal stood a large silver locket encrusted with sparkling gems. By day this would have been a calm and relaxing space, with potential buyers milling around to examine the various works of art. But now, in the dead of night, it was like something from a horror movie.

Theodore Nightstorm was suspended high above the polished marble floor, his limbs bent at impossible angles, legs and arms tangled as if they were made of rubber. As Batman watched, the dealer's body folded in on itself like a sheet of paper being crumpled into a ball before it's thrown in the trash.

No wonder he was screaming . . . although his cries were almost drowned out by another sound—peals of harsh, cackling laughter.

Below Nightstorm was the woman from *The Witch's Trap*, her hands raised high above her head. Her long black hair writhed like snakes around her deathly pale face, those startling blue eyes glittering with malevolence. And now she wasn't screaming. She was grinning wickedly, her hands twisting in the air as she manipulated Nightstorm's limbs, causing more pain with every twisting movement.

Batman had no idea how the woman was alive—or how she was making Nightstorm move in such a terrible manner—but he knew she had to be stopped.

"Put him down," Batman commanded, bursting into the gallery. "Now."

The woman's head snapped around. An amused expression crossed her sharp features as she looked Batman up and down.

"And what are you supposed to be?" she said, her voice dangerously low.

"I am the night," Batman replied, taking a step

forward, "and I cannot allow you to harm that man."

"And *I* cannot allow you to take another step," the woman responded, bringing down one of her arms with a flourish to point at the Dark Knight.

Batman stumbled forward, suddenly unable to move. It was as if his feet had been glued to the floor. But how? Was this magic? Had he just been caught in a spell? It didn't matter. Batman had magic of his own. Pulling a Batarang from his Utility Belt, Batman drew back his arm and let the weapon fly. It spun toward the impossible woman, aiming for her wrist, but she only laughed in amusement.

"You think I am afraid of a little metal bat?" she asked, flicking her long, slender fingers in the direction of the missile. "The creatures of the night are mine to command."

There was a flash of unnatural light and the Batarang changed in mid-flight. One second it was spinning through the air, a thing fashioned of steel by Batman's own hands, and the next it was

flesh and blood, an actual bat, with leathery wings and sharp, pointed fangs. The creature flitted once around the woman before darting back toward Batman, teeth bared.

Another flick of the witch's hand and one bat became many, a swarm of tiny snapping mouths that fell upon Batman, clawing at him and tearing his cape as he tried to protect his face.

"Perhaps now you'll realize the folly of crossing Hilda Grimling, the most powerful witch who has ever lived," the woman crowed as the bats sank their teeth into the Dark Knight's arms. "No one can stop me. Not you, and not that fool of a sorcerer."

"Sorcerer?" Batman asked, trying to buy himself time. "What sorcerer?"

"Augustus Nightstorm," the woman hissed. "He called me evil—and trapped me in a painting for all time. But I escaped—two hundred and fifty-three years to the day that he'd cast his spell— with a common thief taking my place. Only tonight, as the stars aligned on the anniversary of my being trapped in that miserable painting, could I be released. Lucky for me, but not for her. The moment her claws touched the canvas, I was free . . . free to take my revenge on the last of Nightstorm's line."

Grimling threw her hands back up toward the tormented art dealer still suspended in the air.

"You . . . you shall pay for your ancestor's crimes," she said. "You will suffer how I suffered— how no one has suffered before."

But someone is *suffering, and in the same way,* Batman thought from beneath his cape. Selena Kyle was suffering, trapped in the painting that was still slung across his back. For all her crimes, she never deserved that, but how could he rescue her when he couldn't move? How could he rescue Augustus Nightstorm's descendant from a fate worse than death?

Batman tried to jump forward, but his feet were still stuck to the floor. The bats continued to shriek, and Theodore Nightstorm screamed. But were his boots actually still stuck? Had one of them skidded forward, even a fraction? Could he break free?

"You say you're all-powerful," Batman cried

out, fighting to be heard over the noise, "but all I've seen are a few cheap tricks. Conjuring up a flock of bats? Stopping me from moving? What about some real magic? Maybe your powers have gone weak after so many years of hanging on a wall. Maybe you're not the witch you thought you were."

Grimling's face darkened. "Not the witch . . . You have no idea what I can do."

"Then show me!" Batman shouted back. "Show us all . . . unless you're the one who's scared."

"I'm scared of no one!" the witch thundered, rising into the air in front of him, lightning crackling above her fingers. "Not of you. Not of Nightstorm. But now you will share his punishment. You will learn the true meaning of fear."

In an instant, the bats' fangs were the least of Batman's worries. At Grimling's command, a mighty storm blew up in the gallery, with the witch at its center. Paintings were ripped from the walls and they began to spin around and around. Sculptures toppled and crashed to the floor. The locket whipped into the air as its pedestal toppled over. Even the bats were caught in the whirlwind. Lighting flashed and the gale blew as Theodore Nightstorm screamed for help in the unnatural wind.

And Batman's boots moved.

Maybe it was the witch's effort of summoning the storm or the strain of casting so many spells at once, but suddenly Batman was free. The only trouble was that now he had lost his anchor. Batman's cape billowed as he was plucked from the ground, the painting flying from his back to join the others to dance through the air. Batman was thrown into the tempest, his tattered cape flapping as fragments from shattered sculptures and splinters from smashed frames sliced at his arms.

He ignored the pain. He drew his grappling hook and aimed, the barbed hook streaking just in front of Grimling's face.

"You missed," the witch jeered, but Batman knew better. The hook found its target, punching cleanly through the largest canvas that was spinning wildly in the wind. Batman pulled sharply, yanking the painting toward him. Grimling turned a second too late, just as the frame smashed against her, knocking her to the floor, where she landed in a heap. Her concentration was broken, and with it her spells. The storm disappeared to nothing, the other frames dropping out of orbit. Only Theodore Nightstorm remained in the air, still suspended near the ceiling.

Batman pounced, leaping for the witch before she could call on the elemental forces once again. He wasn't quick enough. Grimling swept up a hand and one of the broken paintings leapt from the floor to slam against the Dark Knight. He swatted it away, only to have another work of art fly toward him. And so the fight went; Grimling sending painting after painting zooming toward him, Batman punching and kicking each one away, gaining ground with every passing second.

"You can't win," Grimling screeched, leaping forward to claw at Batman's face before he could reach her. Now it was the Dark Knight's turn to snatch up one of the fallen paintings, using the work of art as a shield. The witch's sharp black-painted fingernails made short work of the canvas, slicing it to ribbons just inches from Batman's face. The Dark Knight threw the frame aside, grabbing another as Grimling continued to advance.

"Soon you'll be back where you belong, Grim-ling," he said, goading her as she tore through the next painting, a once-regal-looking portrait of Gotham's first mayor. "Imprisoned in *The Witch's Trap* for all eternity, just as Augustus Nightstorm had intended."

"Never!" she screamed. "Never will you trap me like he did."

Batman's back bumped against a wall. There was nowhere else to go, and he had only one painting within reach on the floor.

"I never said it would be me," he said, grabbing the last portrait and holding it out in front of him. Grimling raised her hand and struck, slashing viciously.

Her nails never even reached the painting. Instead, a black gloved hand burst from the canvas and grabbed the witch's thin wrist. Grimling's eyes went wide as she realized which painting Batman was holding! Catwoman's angry face glared at her from behind the portrait's brushstrokes.

"No!" Grimling screamed, trying to pull herself

30

free of Catwoman's steely grip. *"The Witch's Trap!* It cannot be!"

But it was. A flash of light blazed from the portrait as the magic of the binding spell reclaimed its prize. The lenses in Batman's mask darkened for a second to protect his eyes from the unearthly light. When the mask cleared again, Grimling was gone. In her place stood Catwoman, who swayed on her feet and slumped to the floor just seconds before Theodore Nightstorm crashed down from the ceiling, released from the witch's spell.

Batman rushed to his side, relieved to see that the art dealer seemed unhurt by his ordeal, his limbs back to normal. The young man only seemed concerned with one thing. . . .

"Grimling?"

In answer, Batman held up his ancestor's painting, which once again showed Hilda Grimling trapped for all time in her enchanted portrait.

Nightstorm shivered and waved the vile painting away. But despite having just escaped with his life from a terrible fate, he didn't seem happy. He immediately began stomping around the gallery, surveying the damage. Not only had many pieces of art been destroyed, but he also quickly realized that the silver locket had gone missing.

"First that blasted book, and now the locket . . . ," he mumbled, clearly agitated about something beyond the mere loss of some expensive items.

"Book?" Batman inquired, raising a quizzical eyebrow behind his mask.

"Nothing. It's nothing," the art dealer responded quickly. He waved Batman away and set about cleaning up his shop as though nothing out of the ordinary had happened.

Batman frowned, turned, and slipped back into the night.

As for Catwoman? Well, Batman had hoped
the experience with the painting would teach the
light-fingered lady a lesson she would never forget,
but when he turned around, Catwoman
was nowhere to be seen.
Neither was the silver locket Batman had spotted
when he'd first arrived at the gallery.
Rumor has it that Ms. Kyle was quite pleased with
herself for having stolen the locket from right under
Batman's nose. No doubt she would have considered
it a *purrr*fect crime....
There was, however, one troubling problem.
The wretched little trinket was jammed shut. But like all
curious cats, she just had to see what was inside.

Eventually, she managed to slip one of her claws beneath

the latch and—*SNAP*—the locket sprang open.

But Ms. Kyle got more than she bargained for.

That locket didn't contain a miniature painting.

Instead, a hideous ghost billowed from the pendant,

released like a genie from a lamp.

Master Bruce says you could hear Catwoman's screams

all the way back to Nightstorm's shop. . . .

Well, one thing is certain: cats may have nine lives,

but those who refuse to learn from their mistakes paint

themselves into a corner, doomed to make the same

mistakes over and over again.

There. That's better. Now
neither of us has to look at that awful scowl.
Out of sight, out of mind.

Oh, you can put the umbrella down now. I really
must throw it away one of these days. Although,
it also has a story, if you'd like to hear it . . . ?

You would?

Excellent.

Well, it will probably come as no
surprise to learn that the umbrella once belonged
to none other than one Oswald Cobblepot.

Yes, The Penguin himself.

That fowl fiend has been a thorn in Batman's side
ever since he first vowed to strike terror into the hearts of
criminals everywhere. They're such a cowardly lot,
you know.

Of course, none of us knew just how much of a
coward Cobblepot was . . . how scared of the
Batman he had become. . . .

TWO

THE BATS IN THE WALL

The night had started like any other in Gotham City: with a crime being committed.

Despite his better judgment, The Penguin had teamed up with Edward Nigma—aka The Riddler—to rob the First Bank of Gotham.

The heist hadn't gone well. The Riddler—as usual—had found it impossible to commit a crime without first leaving a clue for Batman to solve. This time was no different. Soon Cobblepot and

Nigma were on the run from the Batmobile, and it was only a matter of time before the dishonest duo would be brought to justice by the Dark Knight and his young sidekick, Robin.

"Where can we hide?" The Riddler wailed, expecting Batman to strike at any second.

"This way, you question-marked menace," The Penguin quacked, leading The Riddler into an old, condemned building near Crime Alley.

"Are you sure?" The Riddler asked as they walked the crumbling corridors, the floorboards squeaking alarmingly beneath their feet.

"Relax," The Penguin told his panicked partner in crime. They climbed the stairs to the top floor. "This is one of my oldest hideaways. Not even Batman will find us here."

"That's not why I'm worried," The Riddler told him, wringing the rim of his purple bowler hat. "This is the old Abernathy Hotel, right? Everyone knows it's haunted."

"Ack!" The Penguin scoffed, waddling down a long corridor with a grimy window at the far end. "There's no such thing as ghosts."

"No," The Riddler replied as they stopped in

front of a door marked 924. "But there are old mines under this entire neighborhood. Don't you read the papers, Penguin? Just last week, a building like this collapsed into a sinkhole, not two blocks from here. One minute it was there, the next it had vanished into the ground. Riddle me this, Oswald—when is a safe house not safe at all? Answer: When it's a death trap!"

Still, The Penguin wouldn't listen, unlocking the door, which creaked ominously as he pushed his way into the hotel. "That's what *makes* it so safe, you nincompoop. Safe for us!" He closed the door behind him and slammed home not one, not two, but three heavy bolts.

"No one in their right mind would come here," said The Penguin. "You're free to go, Edward, but this is one jailbird who isn't ending up back behind bars." To show that he meant it, The Penguin turned, rapping on the wall of the dirty room with the handle of his umbrella. "There's nothing to fear in the Abernathy. Not ghosts, not the building, and definitely not being found by Batbrain. So which it is? Are you going to stay or go?"

What choice did The Riddler have? He knew

that Batman would strike as soon as he stepped back outside the hotel's dilapidated doors, so he swallowed his fears, looking around at the temporary refuge. Maybe it wasn't so bad. The room was small, sure, and it was hardly luxurious, but there was a bed (which The Penguin immediately claimed) and a sofa.

The plaster was crumbling from the walls, and the windows were boarded up with old planks, but there were candles and even some food . . . old cans of tuna and sardines that The Penguin had stashed here long before. It wasn't much of a supper, but soon The Riddler was curled up like a question mark on the threadbare sofa, snoring softly.

The Penguin tutted and checked the door one last time before he too went to bed, blowing out the candle he'd lit and then climbing onto the lumpy mattress.

But sleep wouldn't come easy. Try as he might, the beaked-nose brute couldn't drop off. He tossing and turned long into the night. The springs in the mattress were the problem, digging into his side every time he tried to get comfy.

And then there were the noises.

The sound of wind whistling down the corridor on the other side of the locked door. The creak of floorboards on the floor above. More the once, The Penguin sat up in bed, convinced that Batman was stalking across the roof, looking for them.

But no Batarangs smashed through the windows. No fists pounded on the doors.

Don't get your feathers in a flap, The Penguin thought. Old buildings creaked. Especially this one. That was why fools like The Riddler thought these buildings were haunted. He and his accomplice were alone. They were safe. No one would find them here.

He rolled over, using his fur-lined coat as a blanket, and tried again to fall asleep. Maybe he would count sardines, like his mumsie had taught him when he couldn't sleep as a child.

One.

Two.

Three.

SCRITCH.

What was that?

The Penguin's eyes snapped open and he stared into the darkness.

SCRITCH. SCRITCH. SCRITCH.

The bed frame groaned beneath The Penguin's weight as he sat up sharply, listening.

What is *that? Where is it coming from?* The

SCRITCH. SCRITCH. SCRITCH. SCRITCH. SCRITCH.

Penguin reached out for the candle on the poor excuse of a bedside cabinet, groping blindly for it in the dark.

The cabinet collapsed and the candle rolled out of sight.

"Wh-what's that?" The Riddler shouted, waking with a start. "Is it Batman? Is he here?"

"It's just the candlestick," The Penguin replied, hauling himself out the bed and abandoning his search. Instead, he activated the flamethrower at the end of his umbrella, sending a spout of flame up toward the cobweb-strewn ceiling.

"Now what are you doing?" The Riddler wailed. "Are you trying to set us on fire?"

"Shhhh!" The Penguin hissed, putting a finger to his thin lips. "I'm trying to listen."

"Listen to what?"

"To that!" The Penguin screeched, spinning around and almost setting fire to The Riddler's hat. "Can't you hear it?"

"All I can hear is you trying to flash-fry every-thing. Turn that thing off!"

Reluctantly, The Penguin complied, his head tilted as he strained to hear the sounds.

SCRITCH. SCRITCH. SCRITCH.

"Something is definitely there. Like tiny claws, scratching."

The Riddler listened for a moment and then shook his head. "There's nothing there. You're imagining it. Go back to sleep." With that, Nigma flopped back over on the sofa with his bowler hat over his eyes.

The Penguin clutched his umbrella, fuming in the middle of the room. *Who does The Riddler think he's talking to, hmm?* It hadn't been The Penguin that had been quaking in his boots about ghosts and sinkholes. And now the puzzle-brained pin-head was accusing *him* of imagining things. And yet . . .

And yet now the room was silent.

The Penguin frowned. The sounds . . . the scratches . . . they had stopped.

The Penguin stood in the darkness, his umbrella held tight in his hands. Perhaps Edward was right after all. Perhaps it was just the darkness playing tricks on him. Everything would seem better in the morning. Yes—yes, it would.

He crawled back onto the mattress, hugging the umbrella to his chest, and finally fell into a restless sleep. He dreamed of monsters climbing

up from the dark, dank foundations of the building, calling his name as they slithered and crawled
toward him. . . . Ossswaaald,
Ossswaaald, Ossswaaald!

SCRITCH. SCRITCH. SCRITCH.
SCRITCH.

The Penguin woke gasping for air. The noises
were back, louder than ever, behind the head-
board . . . behind the walls. Tiny little claws scratching at the woodwork. No, not tiny. Large. Huge.
Monstrous, like in his dream.

SCRITCH. SCRITCH. SCRITCH.

He wasn't imagining it! The monsters were
real! He could hear them as clearly as he heard . . .
as clearly as he heard the voice that now came out
of the darkness.

"He's coming for you, Oswald. The Bat is
coming. He'll find you. *We'll* find you."

SCRITCH. SCRITCH. SCRITCH. SCRITCH. SCRITCH.

That was it. He'd had enough. The Penguin leapt from the bed and almost landed on the sofa, snatching The Riddler's hat from his face.

"What now?" Edward wailed as he was startled awake.

The Penguin grabbed The Riddler by the lapels of his green jacket and poked the tip of his umbrella under the man's chin.

"Why would you say that, you traitorous turncoat?"

"Say what?"

"What you said about the Bat? Are you working with him? Is that what this is all about? Have you sold me out to Batman?"

"I don't know what you're talking about!" The Riddler insisted, pushing the umbrella aside and jumping up from the sofa. "Of course I'm not working with Batman. What's gotten into you?"

Oswald ran his fingers through his lank hair. "They're in the walls. I can hear them. If it wasn't you, it must have been them . . . talking to me, saying that Batman was on his way."

"You were dreaming," said The Riddler. "You said it yourself—this place is as safe as they come. No one will find us here. Not the cops, and definitely not Batman."

But The Penguin wasn't listening. All he could hear was the scratching behind the walls, his name echoing up from the foundations of the hotel!

SCRITCH.
SCRITCH. SCRITCH. SCRITCH.

Oswald! Oswald! Oswald! Oswald!

"Shut up!" The Penguin screamed, whirling around.

"You were the one who started shouting!" The Riddler complained.

"Not you, you fool. The bats . . . the bats in the wall. Can't you hear them?"

"All I can hear is you, birdbrain. Losing your mind."

Maybe that was true. Maybe The Penguin *was*

going insane, but it was the sound of the bats driving him mad, those claws scratching at the plasterwork, trying to get into the room.

SCRITCH. SCRITCH. SCRITCH. SCRITCH.

"I'll show you," he said, pressing the hidden trigger on his umbrella. "I'll show you they're there. Just you see!"

Fire blossomed from the end of the umbrella, burning what was left of the room's faded wallpaper. Fearing that the hotel would burn down around their ears, The Riddler jumped forward, trying to wrestle the umbrella from The Penguin's hand. There was a *crack* and the flames stopped, much to The Riddler's relief and The Penguin's dismay.

"Now look what you've done," the crazed criminal squawked. "Now we'll never be able to stop them. To stop *him*!"

"Just put the umbrella down," The Riddler said, holding out a hand. "It's all going to be okay."

"How can you say that?" The Penguin screeched, launching himself at the blackened wall. "How can you say that when they're in there, clawing their way out?"

And with that, The Penguin swung, smacking his umbrella into the plasterwork. Any other umbrella would have snapped in two with the force of the blow, but The Penguin's umbrellas were always more than they seemed. He slammed it against the wall over and over again, the reinforced shaft clanging like a bell. But still, try as he might, he couldn't drown out the scratching.

The wall finally gave way, the umbrella smashing through the weakened plasterwork. And still The Penguin didn't stop. He tore at the hole with the umbrella's handle. The Riddler jumped aside to avoid being hit by the rubble.

The hole got bigger and bigger and bigger, and . . .

There were no bats.

The Penguin stood panting in front of the hole he had created, breathing heavily and covered head to toe in dust. His head throbbed and his arms felt like lead weights.

Where were the bats?

The Riddler, on the other hand, had another question.

"Have you finished?" he yelled in The Penguin's face. "Or do you want to demolish the rest of the hotel? Why stop there? Why not knock down the entire block! It's not like we need to keep quiet or anything!"

The Penguin stared at the hole in the wall and then looked down at his umbrella. It was now bent in two, broken beyond repair. He had been so sure that there was something behind the wall.

Something monstrous. Something out to get him.

"I getcha, okay?" The Riddler said, his hands raised in front of him, as if worried The Penguin would start beating him now that the wall was smashed. "Being holed up in a place like this, it gets to ya. Especially when you-know-who is out there looking for us. But we're going to be fine. It's all going to be fine."

"You're right," Penguin wheezed, his shoulder slumping. "There's nothing there."

The Riddler nodded, relieved that The Penguin seemed to have regained his senses. "Nothing at all. It was all just in your head. The bats . . . the scratching . . ."

"The voices?"

"*Definitely* the voices. The voices aren't real."

"Not real," The Penguin repeated. "That makes sense. Just my imagination. There's only one problem that I can see. . . ."

"And what's that?"

"If the voices aren't real, why can I still hear them, Edward?"

That was when they came, streaming up from the bowels of the earth, from deep beneath the foundations of the hotel, scraping, scrabbling, crawling, and hissing. Hundreds of sharp claws. Thousands of sharp claws, all desperate to find their prey.

Desperate to find Oswald Cobblepot.

The Penguin screamed as the creatures flew out of the hole, more bats than he could count, their black wings beating and red eyes blazing in the darkness. Too many wings. Too many eyes. They swarmed over him, crawling into his hair,

under his shirt . . . and all the time The Riddler
yelled that nothing was there. The liar!

Couldn't Edward see their hooked claws and
their needle-sharp fangs? Couldn't he smell their
breath? They were everywhere at once, filling the
room. Biting. Scratching. Calling his name.

Oswald! Oswald! Oswald! Oswald!

"I need to get out!" The Penguin screamed,
running for the door.

"Why?" The Riddler cried after him, his voice
muffled by the sound of flapping wings. "What are
you running from?"

"You're working with them," The Penguin
shouted back. "They've got inside your head, but
they won't get into mine."

He was at the door now—struggling with the
bolts, the bats' fangs digging into the backs of his
hands.

"Penguin—don't!" The Riddler screamed, but
he'd already pulled open the door and was racing
out in the corridor. Even then he wasn't free of the
bats. They flowed out into the passageway, turning the air black with their wings. The Penguin ran,

not knowing which way was right and which was left. Was he heading back toward the stairs or toward the cracked window at the end of the corridor?

He didn't care. He just needed to get away from the bats that were calling his name.

The Penguin threw himself through the window and plummeted down, down, down, and the bats burst into the cold night air behind him. They wouldn't leave him alone even as he fell, the wings beating against his head, getting into his eyes. Why wouldn't they stop?

Oswald!

Oswald!

Oswald!

"Oswald!"

Batman's voice cut through the sound of the chirping bats as he swung down and grabbed The Penguin just before he hit the ground. The Dark Knight swung his old enemy back up to safety. It had been Robin who had first heard someone smashing down a wall while they patrolled the street, searching for the Super-Villains. Now the

SCRITCH.
SCRITCH.

SCRITCH.
SCRITCH. SCR

SCRITC

Boy Wonder was in the hotel, cornering The Riddler, who gladly gave himself up. A padded cell in Arkham Asylum was surely better than spending another night with a madman who raved about bats and things that weren't even there.

The Penguin was still raving when he was locked in his cell later that night. The doctors at Arkham had told him that the bats were just a hallucination, brought on by his fear of being captured by the Dark Knight.

The Penguin had nodded, telling the doctors what they wanted to hear. They were right. Of course they were. After all, The Riddler hadn't seen any bats. He hadn't heard them crawling their way out of the walls. He'd feel better after a good night's sleep.

SCRITCH

But he couldn't sleep, not now that the cell door was shut, not as he sat rocking, eyes wide and bloodshot. How could he sleep when he could hear them . . . when he could hear the bats crawling up from the very foundations of the

SCRITCH. asylum, trying to claw their way into his cell.

SCRITCH.
SCRITCH.
SCRITCH
SCRITCH.
SCRITCH.
SCRITC
SCRITCH.
SCRITCH.

Oh, I do beg your pardon.

Something brushed against my cheek.

Perhaps I'm a little nervous, too. The thought of all those bats, ha-ha.

But it was just this, do you see? A harmless scrap of bandage. Maybe it's left over from the last time I had to tend to Batman's injuries after a hard night of fighting crime. It must have caught in a breeze.

The funny thing is that it does remind me of another spooky story that Batgirl once told me. Would you like to hear it, or are you still feeling a little jumpy after our last tale?

You would? Excellent.

You see, it all started with a report in the *Gotham Times*. . . .

THREE

THE SEEDS OF DOOM

READ ALL ABOUT IT! READ ALL ABOUT IT! GOTHAM CITY MUSEUM TO SHOW RARE EGYPTIAN FLOWER!

Rare? The Desert Rose wasn't just rare—it was the talk of the town, at least in historical circles. The pressed flower had recently been discovered in the tomb of Pharaoh Nefarutek in faraway Egypt, sandwiched between layers of papyrus. The flower had bloomed long ago on the banks of the Nile and was thought to have been extinct for over two thousand years.

And yet here was a perfect specimen, its colors as vibrant today as they were in the time of the pyramids. Visitors streamed to the museum to catch a glimpse of the rose, which was displayed in a glass cabinet, their attention piqued by rumors of a curse written on the walls of the tomb. Anyone who tried to steal the ancient bloom would be doomed, stalked by a guardian of the underworld and bound for all time for their crimes.

There were the other treasures from the tomb as well: an army of golden sarcophagi, legions of gem-encrusted statues, and, most impressive of all, a giant golden Sphinx with the adorned head of a woman, the body of a lion, and the majestic wings of a falcon. So much to see and so little time to see it before the exhibition would be packed up and moved on to Metropolis . . . unless, of course, you decided to visit once the doors were locked and the museum was closed to the public. . . .

Gotham City Museum is a spooky place at night, full of shadows and strange noises—not that it worried Frank, the security guard who wandered the halls, checking that the various artifacts were where they should be. On this night, however, Frank's rounds would be cut short.

All was quiet at first as the guard toured the darkened galleries, sweeping his flashlight along the various cabinets and displays. He was just nearing the Egyptology department when he spotted something odd stretching up from a metal grate in the floor. Was that a weed, growing from the floor below? Frank stopped and bent closer, his eyes not being what they once were. Yes. Yes, it was! A delicate weed with small purple flowers reaching up into the corridor.

Frank was sure it hadn't been there when he'd clocked in for his night shift, and . . . and was it moving? Growing before his eyes? Now Frank really couldn't believe what he was seeing. The tiny plant was twisting toward the glow of his flashlight, the flowers opening wider as the beam washed over them. Incredible. Frank got down on one knee to take a closer look and was rewarded by a plume of yellow pollen that enveloped his nose and mouth. His eyes fluttered for a second, and then Frank was asleep before he hit the ground, the halls of the museum soon echoing to the soft rhythm of his snores. And as he slept, the weed continued to grow, creeping through the doors of the Egyptology department and the Desert Rose in its glass case.

Now, no one should have been able to set foot in the exhibition at night, not without setting off the sophisticated security system that protected the artifacts. Lasers crisscrossed the gallery, constantly changing position, so that even Catwoman would have struggled to reach the treasures. But they didn't stop the ever-growing weed that crept beneath the sweeping laser beams and clambered up the walls to a security box. Within seconds, the wriggling plant had curled around the circuitry until . . . CLICK . . . the security system was deactivated.

No more lasers.

No alarms.

The treasures of ancient Egypt were now completely unprotected, although the plant-loving thief who had slunk into the exhibition didn't care for antique gold, crumbling urns, and glistening statues. She had eyes for only one thing. . . .

Poison Ivy stood in front of the Desert Rose's glass cabinet and marveled at its beauty.

"Look at you," she cooed. "So exquisite. So unique. You must be mine."

As she spoke, Ivy raised her arms, and the long weed that had disabled the security system lifted the glass at her command. Smiling in victory, Ivy reached forward to pluck the bloom from its stand, and . . .

"Why don't you keep your green fingers to yourself, Ivy? That Rose belongs to everyone, not you."

Ivy whirled around, her emerald eyes narrowing when she saw who stood in the entrance to the gallery.

"Batgirl," she hissed. "How did you know I was here?"

Batgirl crossed her arms. "Did you really think that was the only security system in the whole museum? An alarm was raised the second your plant knocked out the lasers. You're not taking that Rose, Ivy—not while I can stop you."

"Then it's a good thing that my little darlings can knock out more than a security system," Ivy countered, sweeping an arm toward Batgirl. The weed responded immediately, hurling the glass case toward the Super Hero. Batgirl ducked, and the case smashed against the wall behind her. It had been close, but she wasn't about to wait for another of the weed's tentaclelike vines to strike. Batgirl threw herself toward Poison Ivy, but the weed blocked her, snaking around her legs and lifting her high into the air. Soon the costumed crime fighter was completely cocooned in the binding weed, the vines tightening around her chest. She couldn't stop Ivy from disappearing deeper into the museum with the Desert Rose in her hand.

She could barely even breathe.

Leaving Batgirl to her fate was Ivy's first mistake. The second was not checking the hero's Utility Belt. With a sharp hiss, the vines withered and died, and Batgirl dropped to the floor. She'd stashed a can of fast-acting weed killer in her belt the moment she'd heard that the Desert Rose was going to be displayed at the museum. A rare bloom just ripe for the taking? It would be too much for Poison Ivy to resist.

There was only one problem. The weed was dead, but Ivy was gone . . . as was the Desert Rose. Okay, that was two problems, but Batgirl wasn't beaten yet! Shrugging off the last of the vines, Batgirl headed deeper into the exhibition, creeping past ancient treasures and information boards. The gallery was dark, and the exhibits cast strange shadows in the moonlight streaming through the skylight above her head. Batgirl jumped not once but twice when she turned a corner to find a figure looming out of the darkness in front of her. The first time, it was just a stone statue of the long-dead Pharaoh, and the second time, it was a gilded sarcophagus.

"Keep it together, Barbara," she scolded herself as she crept into the gallery that housed the statue of the golden Sphinx. This wasn't like one of those old mummy movies she'd watched with her dad as a kid. The only monster here was Ivy, and there was no need to get spooked by a room full of ancient artifacts.

But that didn't stop Batgirl's heart from skipping a beat when she realized that the last sarcophagus she'd passed was open! Where was the mummy that was supposed to be resting inside? The casket was empty, with not even a scrap of wrapping to be seen.

Clammy hands grabbed Batgirl's arms. She whirled around, breaking the grip to land a kick in the center of a broad, wrapped chest. Batgirl's mouth dropped open as her attacker stumbled back into the moonlight. It wasn't Poison Ivy. It was the missing mummy, taller than Killer Croc and wrapped head to toe in moldy cloth. How was it moving? Surely it couldn't be alive after all these years!

Alive or not, the mummy swiped for her with

70

a swathed hand. Batgirl ducked, delivering a punch to what would have been the monster's guts if it still had any. The mummy didn't even flinch, lumbering toward Batgirl, and she struck back, dust billowing from the fiend's bandaged arms as they blocked every blow. The ancient horror was unstoppable . . . and worst of all, it wasn't alone.

One by one, the other sarcophagi sprang open, their long-ago mummified occupants shuffling out into the moonlight, shrouded arms reaching for her. Within seconds Batgirl was surrounded, dusty fingers grabbing at her arms and legs. She twisted and turned, but she couldn't break free, and the musty reek of millennia-old cloth was making her gag. But there was something else beneath the rot . . . another smell. Something fresher. Something *perfumed*.

All at once, flowers burst from beneath the mummies' bandages, blossoming yellow, purple, and green. A laugh rang out from the far end of the gallery, and Poison Ivy stepped into the moonlight in front of the sphinx. She had the Desert Rose tucked into her scarlet locks.

"*You're* doing this," Batgirl said, gasping for breath. "*You're* controlling the mummies."

Ivy smirked. "Not the mummies. But the plants within them. I could sense them the moment I stepped into the gallery."

"Seeds trapped within the cloth wrappings during the embalming process," Batgirl said, her detective's mind filling in the gaps. She could imagine seeds and spores in the air becoming part of the layers of cloth, slowly entwined around the bodies during the mummification ritual. "Ready to sprout at your command."

Ivy nodded, her eyes flashing with mischief as she strode toward the trapped crime fighter. "Isn't it delightful? So deliciously macabre. I wish you could have seen your face when my little friends lumbered out of their tombs. You must have thought you'd triggered the Pharaoh's curse."

"I wasn't the one who stole the rose," Batgirl reminded Ivy, her eyes flicking up to the shadows behind the gloating villain. "But I have to say, I'm impressed. Creating puppets out of corpses? That's a good trick. There's only one thing I don't understand. . . ."

Poison Ivy snorted. "There is? Well, let's have it before my bandaged bodyguards give you a nice, tight squeeze."

Batgirl ignored the threat and nodded to the space behind Ivy. "Mummies are one thing, but how are you doing *that*?

Ivy's smile fell away as the floor creaked behind her. She turned, staggering back in shock, her hand going to her mouth. The giant golden Sphinx, once so awe-inspiring on its magnificent pedastal was slowly stalking toward her, its eyes blazing red.

"Who dares disturb the treasures of great Nefarutek?" it boomed, its voice echoing like thunder across the millenia. "Who invokes the curse of the Desert Rose?"

"That's—that's not possible," Ivy stammered, jumping away as a huge golden paw rose over her head, threating to come smashing down.

"It is you!" the monster roared, its scarlet eyes focusing on the stolen bloom in Ivy's hair. "You shall pay for your crimes. You shall be doomed for all time!"

"Not today!" Ivy shouted back, pointing a long

finger at the golden sentinel. "Not ever! Attack!"

At her command, the mummies released Bat-girl and lumbered toward the monster. The Sphinx roared, knocking the first bandaged figure away with a swipe of a gigantic paw. It smashed into a display of funeral urns, reducing the priceless pottery to dust, but the rest of the mummies kept coming. The Sphinx beat its huge wings, but the mummies held on, vines sprouting from the seeds that animated them. Soon the Sphinx was swathed in a green net that tightened around its massive body, its wings flattened and its legs bound tight. With one final bellow, the gigantic guardian crashed to its side, shaking the very foundations of the building as it fell.

Batgirl didn't have to tell Poison Ivy to run. The green-fingered criminal was already racing for the exit, her hand holding the stolen rose in place.

"There is no escape," the downed sentinel growled, opening its mouth and roaring so loud that the skylight above them shattered into a thousand razor-sharp shards. Batgirl threw her cape over her head to protect herself from the falling glass, but she wasn't prepared for the stream of scarabs that spewed from the Sphinx's open mouth. Within seconds, the gallery was filled with the sound of the beetles' buzzing wings, the light from the moon blocked out by a sea of shiny black bodies. Poison Ivy screamed as the bugs swarmed her and the mummies, devouring the plants that bound the Sphinx and descend on Ivy like a plague.

"Get them off me!" the villain cried as the scarabs crawled through her hair, and her remaining mummies blundered around in the storm of ravenous biting beetles. "Get them off!"

"It's the rose they want!" Batgirl shouted as the insects chewed through her cape. "Give it back to them!"

"Never!" Poison Ivy yelled. "It's mine!"

"Then at least give me your hand!" Batgirl called, thrusting her own hand into the swarm. There was no response, save for fingers that closed around Batgirl's glove. *So that's the way you want it,* Batgirl thought, yanking the grappling hook from her belt and aiming for the smashed skylight. She fired, and the hook disappeared into the beetles to wrap around a broken window frame high above. "Hold on!" she said.

Again, Ivy was silent as the line winched them up through the chittering throng and into the cool night sky. With beetles tumbling from her cape, Batgirl flipped over onto the roof, Ivy's hand still clutched in hers.

At least, she thought it was Ivy's hand. Batgirl yelped in horror when she saw cloth-swathed fingers wrapped around her own. It wasn't Ivy's hand, and it wasn't even connected to an arm. Batgirl just saw a yellowed bone sticking out where the wrist should've been.

Batgirl shook off the mummified hand and watched as it tumbled down into the gallery below. It landed with a thud on the museum's polished floor, and Batgirl realized for the first time that the beetles were gone. There was no buzzing, no chewing, no beating wings. In fact, when she leapt back into the gallery, she saw that the mummies had vanished, too, the sarcophagi closed and sealed once more. The giant Sphinx was now on its podium, staring impassively over the exhibit.

And when she ran back through to the entrance, even the Desert Rose was where it should be, displayed in its flawless glass case. Not a thing was

out of place. As if by magic, there was not any sign of the struggle that had taken place.

Batgirl turned, her head spinning. There was no sign of the fight. No sign of any struggle.

And there was no sign of Poison Ivy.

"Hello?" came a voice behind her. "Batgirl? What are you doing here?"

Batgirl turned to find a confused-looking guard standing in the doorway, a flashlight in his hand.

"I don't know what happened," he told her. "One minute I was making my rounds, and the next I was waking up on the floor. I had the strangest dream."

"You're not the only one," Batgirl said, looking back at the Desert Rose.

The guard scratched his head. "What do you mean?"

But Batgirl didn't know. *None of what happened was a dream, was it?* Poison Ivy had been here. She'd stolen the Rose and animated long-dead mummies using the seeds in her bandages. But that didn't explain the Sphinx or the beetles or where Ivy was now.

Batgirl shook her head to clear her thoughts.

Ivy must have escaped when the scarabs had swarmed. Yes, that was it.

There was no way that Ivy was trapped within one of the sarcophagi for her crimes, banging on the lid and screaming to be released.

Because that was the kind of thing that only happened in the movies . . .

As you can imagine, in his line of work, the World's Greatest Detective goes through his fair share of Batmobiles, but this one . . . this one was a particular favorite of mine.

What was that? It looks like it was driven into a wall? Well, there's a very good reason for that. . . .

FOUR

GHOST IN THE MACHINE

"It's the fifth car to be totaled in twenty-four hours," Commissioner Gordon told Batman and Robin, standing beside the mangled wreck of a sports car.

"In the same spot? On the same road?" Robin asked, scratching his head as he looked at the once-beautiful vehicle, its red hood completely flattened against the wall of the newly built Gibson Building in the heart of the city. "What are the odds?"

"Impossibly high," Batman told his inquisitive sidekick—in reality, it was Bruce Wayne's teenage son, Damian. "And all the wrecked cars were stolen?" the Caped Crusader asked, turning back to the commissioner.

"So it seems," Gordon confirmed. "It's been the same every night. The owner leaves their car parked, and the next thing they know, their expensive pride and joy is roaring off into the night, always on the same route. . . ."

"Always with the same end," Batman said, glancing at the wall.

"My officers thought they were going to have to pull the thief out of the wreckage the first time it happened, but when they pried open the door . . ."

"There was no one behind the wheel," Batman mused, remembering the report he had picked up in the Batmobile on the drive from the Batcave.

Gordon sighed. "It's been the same with every crash since."

Robin bent over to look inside the twisted hunk

of metal and whistled. "I'm surprised *anyone* could walk away from a crash like this."

There was no arguing with his logic. The front of the car had accordioned when it hit the wall, pushing the steering wheel into the driver's seat. Anyone in the front would've been pinned in place. And yet the car was empty.

"I'm more surprised that the wall is still standing, after so much punishment," Robin said. "All the cars were traveling at top speed when they hit the building, right?"

This, at least, was something Batman could answer. "The Gibson Building was constructed to survive earthquakes and hurricanes. The walls are reinforced with solid steel. You would need a tank to drive through them."

"Or the Batmobile!" Robin added with a smile.

"Don't even joke about it," The Dark Knight scolded him, turning to face the sound of footsteps. Hurrying toward them was a man wearing an expensive suit and an expression of complete and utter horror.

"Let me through," he wailed when he was

stopped by a couple of burly GCPD cops. "That's my car. My car!"

"*Was* your car," Robin muttered under his breath, only to be silenced by a glare from Batman, whose eyes flicked from the Boy Wonder to a plaque on the wall of the Gibson Building. The distressed owner continued to rant at Commissioner Gordon, wanting to know what the chief of police was going to do about the joyriders who were tearing up Gotham City's streets, wrecking innocent people's cars and putting lives in danger.

"The commissioner is doing everything he can," Batman told the owner, whose face was as scarlet as his *ex*-car, but the man was too angry to listen.

"Yeah? That's easy for you to say. How would you like it if it was your car that was stolen?"

Robin couldn't help chuckling. "Steal the Batmobile? That's impossible."

No sooner had the words left Robin's mouth than he was proved wrong. The Batmobile had been parked across the other side of the street the entire time, but now its headlights flared on and its engine growled. With tires squealing, the car shot forward as if it had a life of its own. An unearthly light glowed from behind its tinted windows and spilled out from beneath its sleek hood. Accelerating wildly, it raced straight toward them. Commissioner Gordon and the terrified car owner were caught in its headlights. The car owner leapt out of the way, but the commissioner didn't have time to move. He was going to be hit by the giant battering ram on the front of the hood!

"Jim!" Batman shouted, throwing himself in front of the speeding car to knock his friend clear. "Look out!"

They hit the asphalt and rolled, and the Batmobile's spinning wheels missing them by a whisker. The car roared on, picking up speed as it disappeared down the street.

"Who's driving that thing?" Commissioner Gordon asked as he pushed himself up, brushing dust from his trench coat. Then he gasped when the Batmobile screamed around the corner to drive the wrong way on a busy thoroughfare!

"I don't know, but they won't get far," Robin

said, jumping onto his motorcycle and gunning the engine.

"Robin, wait!" Batman shouted, but it was too late. The Boy Wonder had already opened the throttle and was speeding away. Batman could only watch as the Red Bird took the corner at speed, Robin's knee nearly touching the ground before he disappeared into the flow of traffic.

"I'll call for backup," the commissioner said, grabbing his radio, but Batman was already shooting a line up to the nearest roof.

"I'm the only backup he needs," the Dark Knight growled as the grappling hook wrapped around a gargoyle jutting out from the building. "You said all the stolen cars have followed the same route?"

Commissioner Gordon nodded. "A lap of the city. Always ending back here."

"Then at least I know where they're going," Batman said as the taut line pulled him up into the night sky.

Horns blared and lights flashed as the Red Bird weaved in and out of traffic. Racing a bike through Gotham City during rush hour was never a good idea, but going the wrong way was even worse! Whatever happened, though, he couldn't lose sight of the Batmobile. The car was barreling ahead at full speed, its tall airfoil fin slicing through the air like a shark's through water. Whoever was behind the wheel wasn't stopping for anyone. Cars swerved out of the way as the black car streaked right down the middle of the road, mounting the sidewalk and smashing past fire hydrants to avoid being knocked from the street.

Robin winced as a delivery truck carrying bottled water careened across the street to avoid driving headfirst into the Batmobile, its cab plowing into a line of vehicles parked along the curb. Chassis buckled and windows popped as the cars were crushed beneath the large wheels, although the danger was far from over.

With the sound of squealing tires, the truck's trailer load jackknifed across the street, but even then the Batmobile didn't stop. It simply smashed through the trailer, its battering ram splitting the load in two. Bottles spilled across the road, shattering on impact, water splashing everywhere. Robin didn't stop, glass crunching beneath his reinforced tires as he pushed the Red Bird to the limit just to keep up. Ahead, the stolen car jumped the lights, with pedestrians scattering to avoid being mowed down. The drivers at the intersection weren't so lucky. Robin had to skid to the right to avoid a sedan that had been run off the road by the speeding joyrider. The sedan crashed into a parked car as sirens blared in the distance.

Finally, Robin thought as Gordon's reinforcements joined the chase, although it was clear that they would never catch up with the Batmobile. With no sign of Batman, Robin had to stop the carjacker himself. Chasing the Batmobile wasn't enough. Robin had to get inside!

The Batmobile took a sharp right, heading down toward the harbor. Robin followed, keeping his eyes locked on the airfoil, and jabbed down on the Red Bird's turbo booster. The bike rocketed forward, screaming toward the Batmobile, with passersby gasping when they thought Robin was going to smash into the speeding car. Instead, the Boy Wonder slammed on the front brake, stopping the Red Bird sharply. The bike bucked, sling-shotting Robin forward. Ignoring the sound of the Red Bird tumbling along the road, Robin flipped over in midair and landed nimbly on the back on the Batmobile, throwing out a hand to steady himself. His cape whipped in the wind as they raced on, blood pulsing in his ears. He had to ignore the fact that they were still driving into traffic at breakneck speed.

Just hanging on was hard enough, especially as the car took another sudden right, going up on two wheels before slamming back down hard. He needed to get inside, needed to know who had managed to steal the most sophisticated car on the planet. Was it one of their enemies, desperate to make a fool of the Dynamic Duo? The Joker, perhaps, or maybe The Penguin? Catwoman had tried to steal the Batmobile on numerous occasions but had never come close. Had she finally gotten lucky, bypassing his father's intricate security systems?

A voice crackled in Robin's ear as he inched forward, broadcast on a secret frequency known only to the various crime fighters of Gotham City.

"Damian, where are you?"

It was his father. Batman sounded like he was running. Was he trying to follow them on foot?

"Where do you think? I'm going for a little spin on the Batmobile."

"*On* it?"

"I'm on the roof," Robin replied, hanging on for dear life as the car took another corner. At least now they weren't driving against the flow of traffic, although that didn't stop the Batmobile from tailgating anyone who wasn't as fast as it was . . . which was more or less everyone on the road! Cars flipped and windshields smashed as they roared on. They must have been going at least a hundred miles an hour, maybe more.

"I'm going to try to get in!" Robin shouted, straining to be heard above both the thrum of the engine and the rushing wind that threatened to throw him from the top of the car.

"Tell me when you're above the cockpit," Batman said over their communicator. "I'll open the canopy remotely."

It was all Robin could do to hang on.

"Do it now!" he shouted back, his fingers slipping.

Batman didn't waste time with a reply. There was a *beep* and the canopy slid back to reveal . . .

. . . nobody! The Batmobile's cockpit was completely empty, with no one in the driver's seat and no one gripping the steering wheel, which suddenly twisted to the right as if steered by invisible hands.

"Aaahhh!" Robin cried out as the car took a corner at a nearly ninety-degree angle. He swung around, tumbling into the cockpit to land upside down in Batman's usual seat.

This time he did reply, calling out in concern.

"Robin?"

"There's no one here," Robin said, struggling to get himself turned the right way up. "The Batmobile is driving itself!"

"That's impossible. Someone must have hacked into the computer, and they're driving it by remote control."

Robin flicked a bunch of switches on the dashboard. "Doesn't look like it. All the systems are working normally, but the pedal is down to the metal and we're accelerating fast."

Above him the canopy suddenly slid shut with a bang.

"Hey," Robin called out. "That's not funny. Why did you close the roof?"

"I didn't," came the reply. "Can you open it from inside?"

Robin pressed the release, but the canopy didn't budge. "So much for all the systems being operational."

He grabbed the steering wheel, but it wouldn't turn. "I can't change direction."

"What about the brakes?"

Robin pumped the pedal. "Not working—and we've almost completed the loop. We're heading back toward the Gibson Building. If we follow the same route as the other cars . . ."

"You'll crash into the wall."

All Robin could think about was the smashed

red sports car with black smoke billowing from its shattered engine.

"The route you've taken *is* interesting," Batman said.

"Not when you're racing to your doom, it isn't!" Robin snapped.

"And that's just what you're a part of," Batman said. "A race. You've followed the route of the first-ever Gotham City Grand Prix, which took place a hundred years agoon this very day. A race that ended in tragedy."

"Then I'd rather that history didn't repeat itself!" Robin shouted, now hammering at the bulletproof windshield with the sole of his boot in an attempt to escape.

"And it's not going to," came the reply just as he heard a thump on the roof.

"Father?" Robin asked.

"I'm on top of the car," Batman told him. "Cover your eyes."

"Why? What are you going to do?"

"Just do as I say for once."

There was a bang, followed by a blinding flash of light. Then the canopy was ripped away, taken by the wind to bounce onto the road in their wake. Robin looked up to see a barbed glove reaching down toward him.

"Take my hand," Batman said.

"But the car . . ."

"No arguments, Robin."

Robin did as he was told, and Batman pulled him back out onto the roof.

"Grab hold of something," the Dark Knight said. "We're taking another corner."

Robin grabbed onto the Batmobile's fin as they swerved right. They were back in the road where the chase had started, racing toward the Gibson Building. Ahead of them, Commissioner Gordon shouted for people to scatter, the wall looming larger by the second as they raced toward it. The cops had moved the wrecked sports car out of the way, but there was nothing to stop the Batmobile from smashing straight into the building.

"Shouldn't we try to stop this thing?" Robin

yelled. "Blow out the tires or something?"

"No," Batman insisted, shaking his head sharply. "That's the last thing we should do."

"*This* will be the last thing we do if we don't jump," Robin told him. The building wall was coming up fast.

"Agreed. On three. One. Two. Three!"

They jumped seconds before the car hit the wall. Robin had been right when he'd said that all the steel plating in the world wouldn't stop the Batmobile. The battering ram did its job, demolishing the side of the building with an ear-shattering crash. Robin turned to the side as dust billowed up, covering the alleyway. When it finally settled, all they could see was a very large hole!

Batman was the first one inside. Robin chased his father to find him standing in front of what was left of the Batmobile. The front of the car had been flattened, smoke billowing up from the engine. The smoke glowed with the same unearthly light Robin had seen in the cockpit.

"It's going to blow!" Commissioner Gordon cried out, running in behind them, but Batman raised a hand to calm his old friend.

"No. Wait."

"For what?" Robin said. "There's no one here. It's . . ."

His voice faded away as a shape began to form in the glowing smoke. Transparent arms . . . legs . . . A full body was floating in the air above the Batmobile. Robin gasped as he found himself staring at the image of a man dressed in old-fashioned racing overalls, with a crash helmet obscuring his face. They watched the apparition reach up and remove the helmet, revealing slick hair and a sharp jaw. The man looked down to them and grinned, nodding in Robin's direction.

"Now, *that* was a race," he said, his voice sounding both near and far at the same time. The specter raised his arms in triumph. The smile remained even as his ghostly body became smoke again and faded from sight as it rose through the ceiling.

"Who was . . . ?" Robin began, not knowing what else to ask.

Commissioner Gordon, however, had another question. "*What* was that?"

"I'll show you," Batman said, leading them out of the building. The plaque he had noticed on the wall was now lying in the rubble on the ground, bent out of shape. The Dark Knight knelt to retrieve the twisted sheet of metal before passing it to Robin.

"'This building is named after Gear Shift Gibson,'" Robin read aloud, "'the famed racing driver who died on this spot before he could complete the first Gotham City Grand Prix.'"

"Good heavens," Commissioner Gordon said, smoothing down his mustache. "I read his story when I was a kid. His engine exploded before he could cross the finish line."

"A finish line that would have been just back there," Batman said, pointing beyond the gaping hole in the wall.

Robin shook his head. "I'm sorry—are you

saying that all those other cars, including the Bat-mobile, were stolen by a ghost so he could finally complete a race?"

"A century after he died," the commissioner added, shivering in the cold night.

"A good detective follows the facts of a case," Batman said, a slight smile playing on his usually somber features. "Unless you have some other theory, Boy Wonder?"

All eyes turned to Robin, but for once the young lad didn't have anything to say.

And Master Damian still doesn't, all this time later. After all, who would believe the story of a spirit taking a car for one last spin, especially a car as special as the Batmobile?

What other explanation could there be?

Now, I don't know about you, but I can't stand around here chitchatting all day. There are a thousand and one jobs to be done. Preparing Mr. Wayne's supper before his nightly patrol. Ironing his capes ...

What's that? You'd like one more story before you go? I suppose we do have a *little* time, but what story to tell?

Ah, yes. I know. Come this way, just beyond the giant penny.

There. A safe bound with chains. Heavy chains, I might add. What do you make of that?

Oh, you think there's something funny about it, do you? You have no idea. . . .

FIVE

THE LAST LAUGH

It all started with a letter pinned to the gates of Wayne Manor one cold Halloween night. Always keen to do my duty, I delivered the missive to Master Bruce, who was sitting with Damian in the main library. They were in front of a roaring fire, preparing for the evening's patrol—and perhaps a bit of trick-or-treating.

There was nothing unusual in the envelope, but the contents appeared to be pages that had been ripped from a book, the edges jagged and torn.

"What kind of book do you think it was?" Damian asked as Master Bruce turned one of the papers over in his hands. The text on the page was bloodred.

"A joke book, by the look of things," Bruce replied. "An extremely corny one, if the gags are anything to go by."

Damian put down the book he'd been reading. "Tell me one."

"Don't say I didn't warn you," Master Wayne said, clearing his throat as the fire continued to crackle in the hearth. "Knock, knock."

"Who's there?" Damian answered, a wry smile playing on his lips.

"Fangs."

"Fangs who?"

"Fangs for letting me in."

Damian groaned. "You're right. That's awful."

But I could tell by the look on Master Wayne's

face that there was more than poor wordplay afoot.

"The next one isn't much better. Why didn't the skeleton go to the Halloween party?"

"I know this one," Damian answered eagerly. "It's as old as Solomon Grundy. The skeleton didn't go to the party because it had nobody to go with!"

Somewhere in Wayne Manor, someone . . . or something . . . laughed.

"Was that Alfred?" Damian asked, but it

wasn't. I was already down in the Batcave, fine-tuning the Batmobile for the Dynamic Duo's next mission.

"Why don't you read another?" his father said, passing the scrap of paper to his son.

Damian took it, and for once did as he was told. "Did you hear about the ghost who robbed a bank?" he asked.

"Let me guess," Bruce said gravely. "It was a polter-heist!"

The laughter got nearer. . . .

The jokes continued, with Damian setting them up and Bruce knocking them down.

"Why are graveyards so noisy?"

"Because of all the coffin."

"What do witches race on?"

"Vroom-**sticks!**"

"How do ghosts keep their spooky hair in place?"

"They use scare spray!"

And all the time, the laughter got louder and closer and sounded more berserk.

Damian leapt up from his seat when a group of giggling ghosts appeared in the library, each dressed as a creepy clown with bone-white skin and a bloodred nose. Their eyes flashed with monstrous mirth as their mouths split into grins that revealed row upon row of needlelike teeth.

But as scary as they looked, it was the laughter than made the crime fighters' skin crawl. It rattled the panes in the windows and made the books on the library's shelves shake so violently that they dropped to the floor.

The more the ghosts laughed, the more that others appeared, some with chortling pumpkins for heads and others little more than filmy skin and bones. Soon the library was filled with them, the snickering specters clutching their transparent sides as if they might burst.

They swept forward as one, forcing Master Bruce and Damian back toward the ornate stone fireplace. Damian swung a punch, but his fist slipped through the nearest spook as if it weren't there, which made it laugh even more.

"Sooo funny!" the spirit shrieked at the look of surprise on the young crime fighter's face. "I could laugh my head off."

"And me," said the next ghoulish jester.

"And me too," agreed the next, until that was exactly what they did, their translucently pale

bodies shaking so much with laughter that their horrific heads toppled from their shoulders, exploding like firecrackers as they hit the floor.

And still more ghosts appeared, crowding forward, their sides splitting to show the ribs that

had been so tickled by the infernal puns.

"This is beyond a joke!" Damian cried, his hands pressed tightly over his ears to block out the terrible noise.

Master Bruce's eyes went wide as he realized what was happening. "That's it, Damian. It was the jokes that brought them here."

"Well, it's not very funny!" Damian yelled back.

"Quick!" Master Bruce shouted, barely able to make himself heard over the horrible hilarity. "Throw the page into the fire!"

"What?"

There wasn't much time, so Master Bruce yanked the page from Damian's hand and tossed it into the hearth. The paper flared with supernatural light the moment it hit the flames. It was so bright that Damian had to squeeze his eyes shut to avoid being blinded.

But when Damian opened his eyes again, the library was calm and empty—although his ears were still ringing from the sound of the ghastly laughter. It took him a moment to realized what had happened. The ghosts had all burst into puffs of smoke and ash.

"Are you all right?" Damian's father asked, looking with concern at his son.

"I am, now that we can hear think ourselves think. I know it's Halloween, but that trick was no treat!"

Just then, a chime rang out from deep inside Wayne Manor. It was the Batcomputer indicating a call from Commissioner Gordon.

Across Gotham City, Theodore Nightstorm was in his storeroom, cataloging his latest acquisitions, when he heard the creak of a floorboard in the gallery at the front of the building. *That's odd,* he thought. *I was sure I locked the front door.* The memory of his recent experience with Hilda Grimling was all too fresh in his mind. He put down his pen and closed his recordkeeping notebook, picking it up to test its weight. He doubted it would be of much use against an angry witch, but he wasn't about to venture out into the darkness on this Halloween night, of all nights, without something to defend himself.

He crept slowly toward the door that led to the gallery, listening intently. Someone was definitely out front. He could feel their presence in the still air, goose bumps prickling on his arms.

"Hello?" he called, brandishing the book like a shield. "I have to warn you, I'm armed."

"You won't need weapons against us," came a grim voice on the other side of the door. "Not if you answer our questions."

Nightstorm's mouth dropped open.

"Batman?"

The art dealer pushed open the door to see two figures standing in the darkened gallery: the imposing silhouette of the Caped Crusader with his faithful partner, Robin, at his side.

"You gave me quite a fright," Nightstorm said, tucking the notebook under his arm.

"You're not the only one to get spooked tonight," Robin told him, crossing his arms across his young chest. "People have been scared all across the city!"

"It is Halloween, I suppose," Nightstorm said, still not sure why the caped crusaders were there.

"A night for spooky stories from spooky books," Batman said, stepping out of the shadows. "Maybe like the one you mentioned when I was last here."

Nightstorm's brow furrowed. "I'm not sure I know what you mean."

"You told Batman that a book had been stolen," Robin explained. "Part of your collection?"

"Ah, yes," said Nightstorm. "The Necro-comicon. A curious tome, indeed."

"Necro what, now?" Robin asked.

Nightstorm's face turned grave. "The Joke Book of the Dead."

The Boy Wonder snorted in disbelief. "The Joke Book of the Dead? You're kidding me!"

"The Necrocomicon is no laughing matter, I assure you," Nightstorm told him. "It was written ages ago by an unknown hand, filled with gruesome gags and dark humor."

"I told you the jokes were old," Robin said, glancing at his masked mentor.

"You know where it is?" Nightstorm asked eagerly.

"No, but we hope you can help locate it," Batman said. "Tonight a number of important people in Gotham City received pages torn from what we think is your missing book."

Nightstorm's face went as white as the ghosts that had haunted Wayne Manor not an hour before. "Torn? Pages were torn from the Necro-comicon?"

"We think so. When the . . . victims read the jokes out loud—"

"They were tormented by laughing specters," Nightstorm said, loosening his collar. "I've been afraid something like this would happen ever since the book first went missing. Who received the pages?"

"The head of Wayne Industries and his son," Robin told him.

"Plus Commissioner Gordon, the mayor, and a few more of Gotham City's prominent citizens," Batman added. "Everyone was rattled and terrified, and no one is likely to sleep the next few nights, but they're mostly fine otherwise. We've gathered all but one of the pages, which was burned to banish the ghosts, but we need to track down who sent the pages before they strike again."

"I wish I could help you," Nightstorm said.

"But the book was stolen weeks ago. I've no idea who took it, unless . . ."

"Unless what?" Robin prompted as the art dealer's voice trailed off.

"I did have one customer on the day the Necrocomicon went missing. A woman with the palest face I've ever seen."

Batman leaned in at the description. "Pale? What about her hair? Was it dyed?"

"Dyed?"

"Red and black," said Batman.

Nightstorm shrugged. "There was no way to know. It was swept up beneath her hat, you see— a rather curious affair, so she looked like a medieval jester."

The Dynamic Duo exchanged a knowing look.

"Oh, she did say she was looking for a present for someone named Mr. Jay," Nightstorm said, remembering one last detail about the curious customer. "Does that help?"

"More than you know," the Dark Knight rumbled as he turned and swept out of the gallery, with Robin following close behind.

Even on the spookiest night of the year, no one in their right mind went near the abandoned fun fair on Gotham Harbor. The place had shut its gates decades before, its once-thrilling rides now rusted beyond repair and its gaudy attractions faded and broken. No lights twinkled or music played, except for one dilapidated building at the heart of the fair.

Once upon a time, the fun house had delighted the children of Gotham City, but now it served as a hideout for the city's most infamous villains. The laughter that echoed through its hall of mirrors wasn't the macabre mirth of a sniggering spirit, but rather the creepy cackles of the Clown Prince of Crime himself—The Joker—and his chaos-loving partner in crime, Harley Quinn.

This evening, however, Harley couldn't figure out what The Joker was finding so funny. She'd done what Mr. Jay had asked, swiping the spooky-looking book from that stuffy old art gallery and delivering it to The Joker's chalk-white hands. He hadn't wasted a second, immediately ripping page after page from the leather-bound book and getting them ready to be mailed to all four corners of Gotham City.

She had no idea what he was up to, which, if she was honest, wasn't all that unusual. The Joker wasn't known for explaining his madcap schemes, but once in a while, she liked to be in on the joke.

"C'mon, puddin'," she complained and pouted as The Joker gleefully rocked back and forth on his heels. "I thought you said we were gonna have some Halloween fun."

"And we will, my dear." The Joker giggled. "We will. Much more than those boring old stiffs in City Hall. Or the police department. Or even Wayne Manor. We've spread a little Halloween cheer, you see. Raised a few spirits, you might say."

Once again, The Joker dissolved into a fit of giggles.

"Well, I don't get it," Harley complained, "and I'm not spending my favorite night of the year cooped up in this old ruin. I need to show everyone my costume."

At least that made The Joker stop. "Why?" he said, looking her up and down. "What have you dressed up as?"

"Me, of course," Harley said, giving him a twirl. "What could be scarier?"

"What indeed?" boomed a voice. Harley spun around in shock. Most sane folks stayed away from their hideout.

"Who's that?" she asked, snatching up her oversize mallet.

"Trick or treeeeat!" sang another voice from somewhere near the gag staircase. "Which do you want?"

Now it was The Joker's turn to whirl around and shout into the darkness.

"I'm the only one who plays tricks around here, buster!" he snapped, the tattered Necrocomicon held tightly in his hands.

"We just wanted to put a smile on your face," the deeper of the two voices said. "Maybe tell a spooky joke or two."

"Here's one for you now," said the younger voice. "Knock, knock."

"Oh, no," The Joker said, his face whiter than ever. "No, no, no, no!"

"What's wrong?" Harley asked as The Joker hugged the Necrocomicon to his narrow chest. "It's only a gag. We like gags, right?"

"Knock, knock," the voice repeated growing impatient.

"Who's there?" Harley shouted back.

"No! Don't!" The Joker snapped, turning on her. "You don't understand what you're doing."

"I'm answering the joke," Harley said. "That's what you do. Someone says, 'Knock, knock,' and you say, 'Who's there?'"

"Boo," came the reply.

Harley grinned from ear to ear. *Now, this is fun.*

"Boo who?" she shouted.

"No need to cry," the younger voice replied. "We only want some candy."

A howl of laughter rang through the house of fun.

"That's more like it, huh, Joker," Harley said,

turning back to her usually giddy partner in crime. "Let yourself go."

But for once, The Joker wasn't laughing. In fact, he was running for the exit.

"Hey, where are you skeddaddlin' off to in such a hurry?" she asked.

He didn't reply. Instead, he almost squeaked in terror as another joke thundered out, followed by another, and another. Harley knew the answer to each one.

"What's a vampire's favorite fruit?"

"Neck-tarines!" she shouted, laughing.

"What do vegetarian zombies eat?"

"G-g-grains!"

"How do you make a witch itch?"

"Take away the *W*!"

By now Harley was laughing so hard, she could barely stand. And The Joker hadn't gotten out the door. When he'd thrown it open, he was greeted by a ghostly clown. And more of them came through the door with every joke Harley answered. New clowns appeared, the grins on their faces showing leering skulls just beneath the surface.

Their laugher echoed louder and louder from the dark corners.

It was only when The Joker screamed—and not in the fun way Harley was used to—that she

realized what was happening, and by then it was too late. The fun house was teeming with snickering shades and guffawing ghosts, each one more terrifying than the last. Things suddenly weren't so funny as she swiped at the nearest spook and her mallet passed straight through the phantom's pumpkin head as if it weren't there!

And still the jokes kept coming, puns almost as terrible as the laughter that bounced from the fun house's crooked walls.

"What did the monster eat after its teeth were taken out? The dentist!"

"How do ghouls like their bacon? Terri-fried!"

"What do witches learn in high school? Spelling!"

The Joker could take no more. "Make it stop! Make it stop!" he wailed as the ghostly clowns crowded around him with their terrifying laughter.

HA HA HA HA HA
HA HA HA HA HA
HA
HA HA HA
HA HA HA
HA HA HA
HA
HA HA HA
HA HA HA-HA
HA HA HA HA HA HA
HA

He threw Necrocomicon, but it didn't do any good. Like Harley's mallet, it sailed straight through the laughing ghoul. Harley leapt to grab it,

but something got there first, a dark shadow dropping from the ceiling to snatch the book in a black-gloved hand.

And still the ghosts laughed.

Harley couldn't see who had grabbed the book. She couldn't see anything but the specters that crushed in from all angles, their breath as stale as the gags in that old book.

HA HA HA

And more jokes . . .

What's a spook's favorite type of tree?

Ceme-trees!

HA HA HA HA HA HA

Why did Dr. Jekyll cross the road?

To get to the other Hyde!

Who did the monster take to the Halloween dance?

"His ghoul-friend," Harley answered, unable to help herself, even as the ghost clowns pushed in on her and The Joker.

"Now, Robin! Do it now!"

Somewhere above her, Harley heard the sound of paper being torn into tiny pieces. She didn't care. She was too busy screaming as the ghosts exploded into puffs of glitter and confetti right before her eyes.

And then they were gone. No ghosts, no spooks—only Batman standing over her, Mr. Jay's ratty old book in his hands. Harley looked up to see little scraps of paper drifting down like snow from where Robin had been hiding in the rafters high above their heads.

"Confetti!" Harley said gleefully, her fear strangely already forgotten as she reached out to punch The Joker in his shoulder to see if he was seein' what she was seein'. But The Joker was curled up in a ball and crying with fear . . . with terror.

"Guess the joke's on Mr. Jay, eh, Bats?" Harley said as she looked up at the Dark Knight.

You see, the ghosts were finally all gone, but The Joker could still hear their laughter . . . that dreadful manic laughter . . . forever in his head. . . .

Oh, dear. Well, there's

nothing funny about your complexion.

You've gone as pale as a ghost yourself.

Perhaps that ending was a little on the grisly side,

but do not fear—what remains of the Necrocomicon is

locked safely within this vault, never to be seen again.

But now it really is time for you to go, my young

friend. I promised you one last story, and that was it.

Of course, if you enjoyed my chilling tales of ghoulish

Gotham City, then maybe you'd like to come back another

dark and stormy night for more stories?

You would like that? Good. So would I.

I'll show you out ... but wait ... goodness me, the sheet

has fallen from *The Witch's Trap*.

Will you just look at the dust on that frame? That

will never do. I'll just grab my feather duster and

give it a little flick before we—

It's Grimling! She's got my duster! She's got me!

Run! Run as fast as you can! I'll see you next time for more tales from the Batcave.

There will be a next time . . .

... won't there?